Another Sommer-Time Story™

Three Little Pigs

By Carl Sommer
Illustrated by Greg Budwine

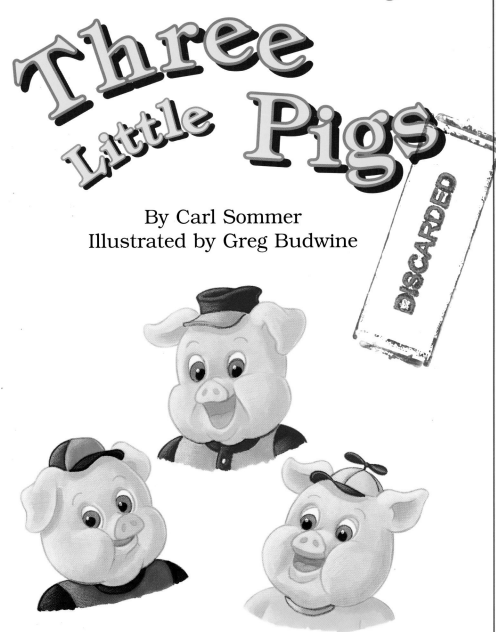

 Advance PUBLSHING, INC.

Permissions
Advance Publishing, Inc.
6950 Fulton St.
Houston, TX 77022

www.advancepublishing.com

First Edition
Printed in Singapore

Library of Congress Cataloging-in-Publication Data

Sommer, Carl, 1930-
    Three Little Pigs / Carl Sommer: illustrated by Greg Budwine. -- 1st ed.
        p. cm. -- (Another Sommer-Time Story)
    Summary: Three little pigs leave home to seek their fortunes and have to deal with a threatening wolf.
    Cover title: Carl Sommer's Three Little Pigs.
    ISBN 1-57537-011-5 (hardcover: alk. paper). -- ISBN 1-57537-063-8 (library binding: alk. paper)
    [1. Folklore. 2. Pigs Folklore.] I. Budwine, Greg, ill. II. Three Little Pigs. English. III. Title. IV. Title: Carl Sommer's Three Little Pigs. V. Series: Sommer, Carl, 1930- Another Sommer-Time Story.
PZ8.1. S6654Li 2000
398.24'529633   99-35281
[E]--dc21   CIP

Three Little Pigs

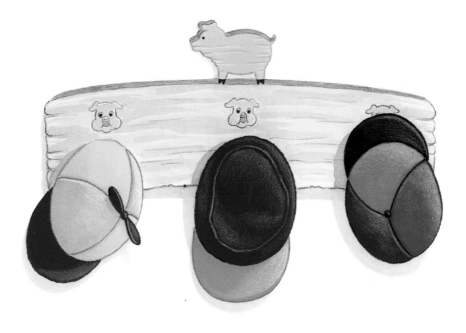

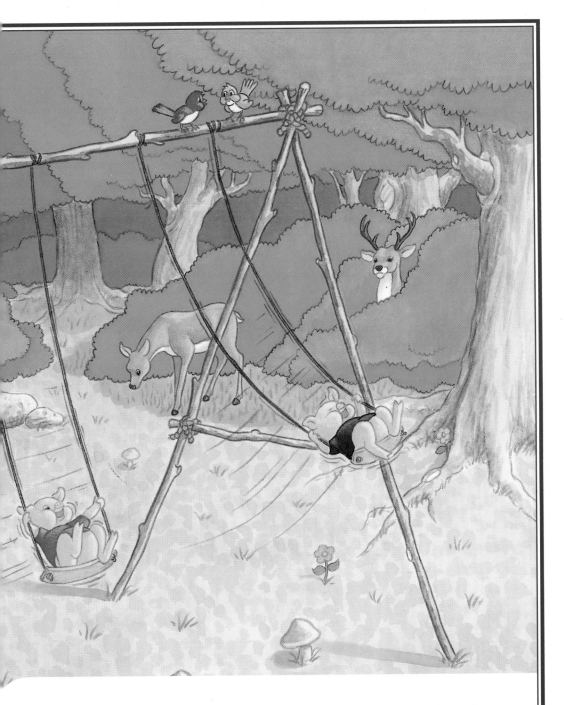

Long, long ago in a forest far away there lived a happy family of pigs. There was Papa Pig, Mama Pig, and the three little pigs, Dozey, Pokey, and Hardy.

The three little pigs grew big and strong. Both Papa and Mama had taught them many things. But Dozey would rather do anything than listen to Papa and Mama teach.

Whenever Papa or Mama gave Dozey work to do, he would always complain, "I don't want to work. I want to play."

Whenever Papa or Mama gave Pokey work to do, he would obey. But after a short while he would grumble, "This is hard work! I'm quitting!"

But whenever Papa or Mama gave Hardy work to do, he always listened and obeyed. And even when things got hard, Hardy kept working and working.

The three little pigs grew and grew. Finally the time came for them to go out on their own.

Before they left, Papa gave them a strong warning. "Make sure you build a sturdy house. If you don't, the big bad wolf can get you. And don't forget to study to learn how to build a sturdy house."

"Okay, Papa," said Hardy and Pokey.

Dozey just yawned. He would never study, for thinking was work. Anyway, he already knew all he needed to know.

After getting lots of hugs and kisses from Papa and Mama, the three pigs waved goodbye.

Dozey decided to build a house quickly. He gathered some straw and built his house fast.

As Dozey looked at his house, he stuck out his chest and said, "Look at the fine house *I* built. See, I didn't have to waste my time and study."

Now Dozey no longer had to work and think; he could do what he liked—relax and play.

Pokey wanted to obey Papa and Mama and build a strong house, but he did not know how. "Maybe I should go to the library and learn about building houses," he said to himself.

But when he found out that the library was far away, he said, "I don't need a library. I can figure out by myself how to build a strong house."

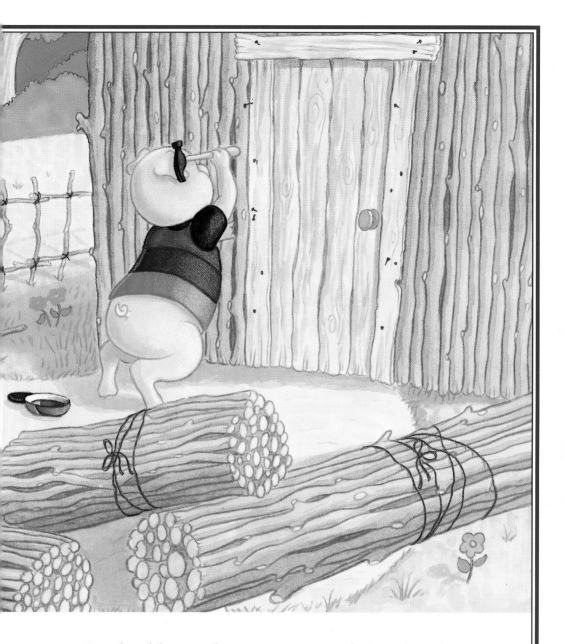

But building a house was much harder than he thought. As the sun beat down on Pokey, he became hot and tired.

He looked over at Dozey's house and groaned, "I give up! Dozey is already finished. I'll just quickly finish my house. I can always build a stronger house later when it's not so hot."

"Hooray!" yelled Pokey as he hammered the last nail into his house. "I'm so glad I'm finished!"

He quickly got out his lawn chair and lay down to relax under a big tree. Then Dozey came over to compliment him. "Good job, Pokey! Now you too can relax and play."

Meanwhile, Hardy was barely getting started. Every day he had taken a long walk to the library to learn how to build a strong house.

After he learned how to build a strong house, he went to the store and bought the proper tools and materials.

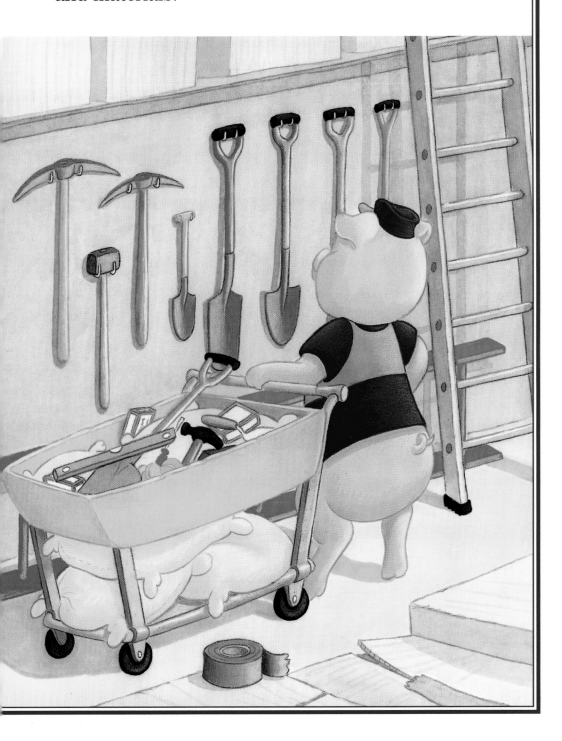

At last it was time to build. Hardy began by digging his basement. The ground was dry and hard. The sun beat down on him, and sweat poured down his face.

"This isn't going to be easy!" said Hardy as he wiped the sweat from his brow.

But he had made up his mind that no amount of hard work would stop him from building a strong house.

Dozey, who had just awakened from his nap, came strolling by.

"Why don't you be smart and build a house like mine?" yawned Dozey. "That way you won't have to work so hard. Then you too can relax and play."

"Oh no!" said Hardy. "I'm building a strong house. Remember, Papa and Mama warned us about the big bad wolf."

As Hardy began mixing cement to lay the bricks, he got another visitor—Pokey.

"You're working much too hard," warned Pokey. "You need to learn to relax and play. Build a house like mine. You can always build a strong house later when it's not so hot. Why don't you come and play with us?"

"Oh no!" said Hardy. "I'm building a strong house *now*. Remember, Papa and Mama warned us about the big bad wolf."

The next day both Dozey and Pokey came to watch Hardy work. "Ha! Ha! Ha!" they teased. "We've already finished building our houses, and we're having lots of fun. Ha! Ha! Ha!"

"You can laugh at me," said Hardy, "but I'm listening to Papa and Mama."

Dozey and Pokey walked away laughing as they hurried off to play.

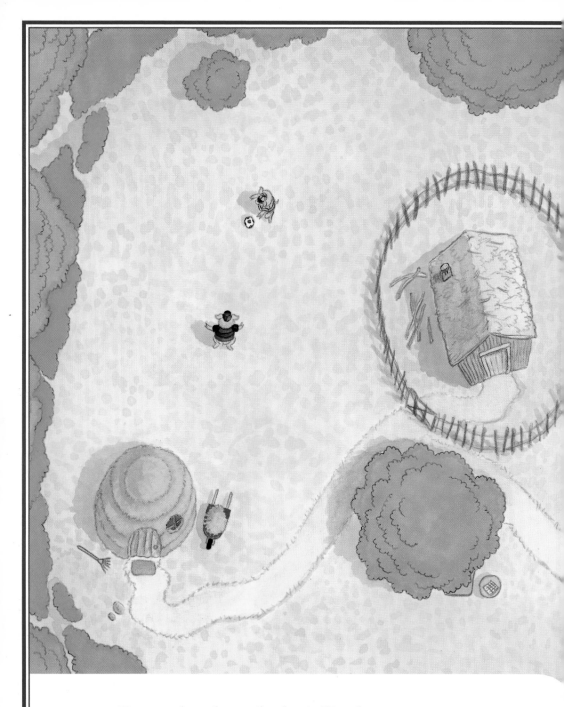

It was hard work, but Hardy never gave up. He had built his house just like the books had told him. As he looked at his sturdy house, he said, "I'm so glad I didn't give up."

Although Hardy's house was finished, he was not ready to play. "I have to do one more thing," he said to himself.

Just then there was a knock at the door. It was Pokey and Dozey.

"Ready to play now?" Pokey asked.

"Not yet," said Hardy as he walked out the door. "I'm going to the library."

"Library?" shouted Dozey and Pokey in amazement. "Don't be so foolish. You need to learn to stop working and studying so hard. Be like us and have some fun!"

But Hardy paid no attention to them. He waved goodbye and went straight to the library.

At the library, Hardy looked for books about wolves. He wanted to find a way to get rid of the big bad wolf once and for all.

Hardy searched and searched. Then his eyes lit up. He had found the answer!

"If that big bad wolf tries to get me," he said to himself, "I'll know just what to do."

One day the big bad wolf did come. He was creeping through the woods looking everywhere to find something to eat.

"Grrrrrrr!" he growled. "I'm starving! I have to find something to eat!"

While prowling through the forest, suddenly the wolf came upon a clearing. He saw three little houses... and one little pig. "Mmmmm! Mmmmm!" he said as he licked his lips. "That

little pig will make a perfect meal."

His mouth began to water as he headed toward the little straw shack. When Dozey saw the wolf, he ran inside. He shook all over, for he knew his house was not strong enough to keep out the big bad wolf.

"Ha! Ha! Ha!" laughed the wolf when he came near the house. "I'll blow that house down with just one little puff."

"Wh-wh-what should I do?" cried Dozey as the hungry wolf came to search his house. Then Dozey got an idea.

When the wolf reached the front of the house, Dozey dashed through the back wall of his house, running as fast as he could to Pokey's house.

"Let me in! Let me in!" yelled Dozey as he pounded on the door. "The big bad wolf is coming!"

Quickly, Pokey opened the door, and Dozey rushed inside. They went straight to the window. Dozey was shaking all over as he watched the big bad wolf, with just one little puff, blow his house down.

"Ohhhhhh!!!" cried Dozey. "How foolish of me to build such a flimsy house."

The wolf searched through the rubble, but he could not find Dozey. "He must be next door," the wolf grumbled.

When Pokey saw the wolf coming, he cried, "What can we do? This house isn't strong enough to keep out that wolf!"

Suddenly, the wolf began to huff and puff at Pokey's wobbly house. Each time he huffed and puffed, part of the house blew away.

"My house is falling apart," groaned Pokey. "What should we do?"

"I know what we can do!" whispered Dozey. "Each time the wolf huffs, he closes his eyes. Let's run to Hardy's house the next time the wolf begins to huff!"

"Great idea!" said Pokey.

When the wolf began to huff, they quickly opened the back door and raced to Hardy's house.

When they came to Hardy's house, they yelled as loud as they could, "Let us in! Let us in! The big bad wolf is after us!"

But there was no answer, and the door was locked. "Hurry up, Hardy!" they screamed. "Let us in!"

Still, no answer. "Oh, no!" cried Dozey. "He's not home!"

They looked around and saw the roof fly off of Pokey's house. Then the wolf blew again, and the rest of the house came down.

"Ohhhhh!!!" moaned Pokey. "There goes all my hard work."

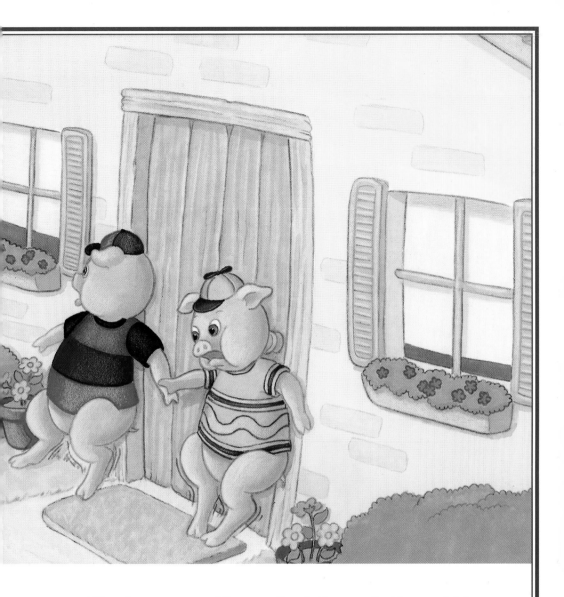

The hungry wolf searched through the rubble for Dozey and Pokey, but he could not find them. Now he was not only hungry—he was mad—very mad.

"I'll catch them yet!" snarled the wolf as he headed straight for Hardy's house.

"Oh no!!!" cried Dozey. "The big bad wolf is sure to get us now!"

Suddenly, Dozey turned and shouted, "Look!"

It was Hardy opening the gate. "Hi, Dozey and Pokey," he called. "What's—?"

"Hurry!!!!!" they screamed. "The big bad wolf is coming!"

Hardy turned and spotted the wolf. He raced for the door. The wolf jumped over the fence and ran towards them.

Hardy threw open the door, and they dashed inside.

In a flash, the wolf was at the house, but he was too late. Hardy slammed the door in his face. And before the wolf could blink, Hardy bolted the door shut.

Now the wolf was furious. "You won't get away from me this time!" he roared. "I'll blow this house down just like the other two. Then you'll have no place to run!"

He braced himself and took a deep breath. Suddenly, a mighty blast of wind ripped across the little brick house.

But nothing happened.

He huffed and puffed and blew again. Leaves
and branches flew off the trees. Garden tools
and fence boards flew everywhere, but nothing
happened to the house.

The wolf huffed and puffed . . . and huffed and
puffed some more! He huffed and puffed so hard
that his insides hurt. But with all his huffing
and puffing, he could not blow the house down.

"You did it!" shouted Pokey. "You did it! You built a house that's stronger than the big bad wolf!"

"Hooray!" yelled Dozey. "Now he'll finally leave us alone!"

"I don't think so," answered Hardy as he hurried into the kitchen. Hardy had read all about wolves, and he knew that this wolf was not about to give up.

Hardy was right. The angry wolf walked up to the house, and with a single leap, jumped on the roof. He began to scratch, jump, and pound on the roof. "I'll show them," he said. "I'll make a hole in the roof, and then I'll crawl through."

But the roof was much too strong to crush. Then he sat down to decide what he should do next. "I'm not giving up!" he growled.

The wolf thought and thought. Then he let out a wicked laugh, "Ha! Ha! Ha! I'll surely get them now! I'll just slide down the chimney."

The proud wolf, grinning from ear to ear, began to climb down the chimney.

"I'll get you now!" he shouted down the chimney. When Dozey and Pokey heard the wolf, they dashed into the kitchen to get Hardy.

Hardy was standing by the stove.

"Hardy!" cried Pokey and Dozey. "The wolf is going to get us! This is no time to prepare a meal for us!"

But Hardy was not cooking. He had prepared a surprise for the wolf . . . a big pot of boiling water.

Just as Hardy put the big pot into the fireplace, the big bad wolf slid right into the boiling water!

There was one loud yell, and that was the end of the big bad wolf.

The three pigs ran outside and danced for joy. "I'm so glad you listened to Papa and Mama and built a strong house," Dozey told Hardy.

"I'm sure glad you *didn't* listen to us!" said Pokey.

"I am too," laughed Hardy. "But now that the wolf is gone, let's have some fun and play ball."

"Oh no!" said Pokey and Dozey. "We have work to do!"

Off they went to build new, strong houses, just like Hardy's. They had learned their lessons—listen and work hard.

And that is why they lived happily ever after.

Read Exciting Character-Building Adventures
★★★ Another Sommer-Time Stories ★★★

**Coming!
Spanish Bilingual
Editions**

**Coming!
Another Sommer-Time
Adventures on DVDs**

Available as Read-Alongs on CDs or Cassettes

Visit www.AdvancePublishing.com
For Additional Character-Building Resources